S0-AGU-088

Up and Down the Andes
A Peruvian Festival Tale

For my godchild, Madeleine – L. K.

Pour mes parents Laura et Alexandre, et pour mes enfants chéris Anouk et Mathis – A. F

Barefoot Books
2067 Massachusetts Ave
Cambridge, MA 02140

Text copyright © 2008 by Laurie Krebs Illustrations copyright © 2008 by Aurélia Fronty
The moral right of Laurie Krebs to be identified as the author and Aurélia Fronty to be identified as the illustrator of this work has been asserted

First published in the United States of America in 2008 by Barefoot Books, Inc.
This paperback edition published in 2011
All rights reserved. No part of this book may be reproduced in any form or by any means,
electronic or mechanical, including photocopying, recording or by any information
storage and retrieval system, without permission in writing from the publisher

This book has been printed on 100% acid-free paper

Graphic design by Louise Millar, London
Color separation by B & P International, Hong Kong
Printed and bound in China

ISBN 978-1-84686-468-1

This book was typeset in Infilto and Aunt Mildred
The illustrations were prepared in acrylics

3 5 7 9 8 6 4 2

The Library of Congress cataloged the first hardcover edition as follows:
Krebs, Laurie.
  Up and down the Andes : a Peruvian festival tale / Laurie Krebs, Aurélia Fronty.
     p. cm.
  ISBN 978-1-84686-203-8
  1. Inti Raymi Festival--Juvenile literature. 2. Indians of South America--Andes Region--Social life
and customs--Juvenile literature. 3. Festivals--Andes Region--Juvenile literature. 4. Andes Region--
Social life and customs--Juvenile literature. I. Fronty, Aurélia. II. Title.

  F2230.1.S7K74 2008
  394.26598'32309853--dc22

                                    2008020722

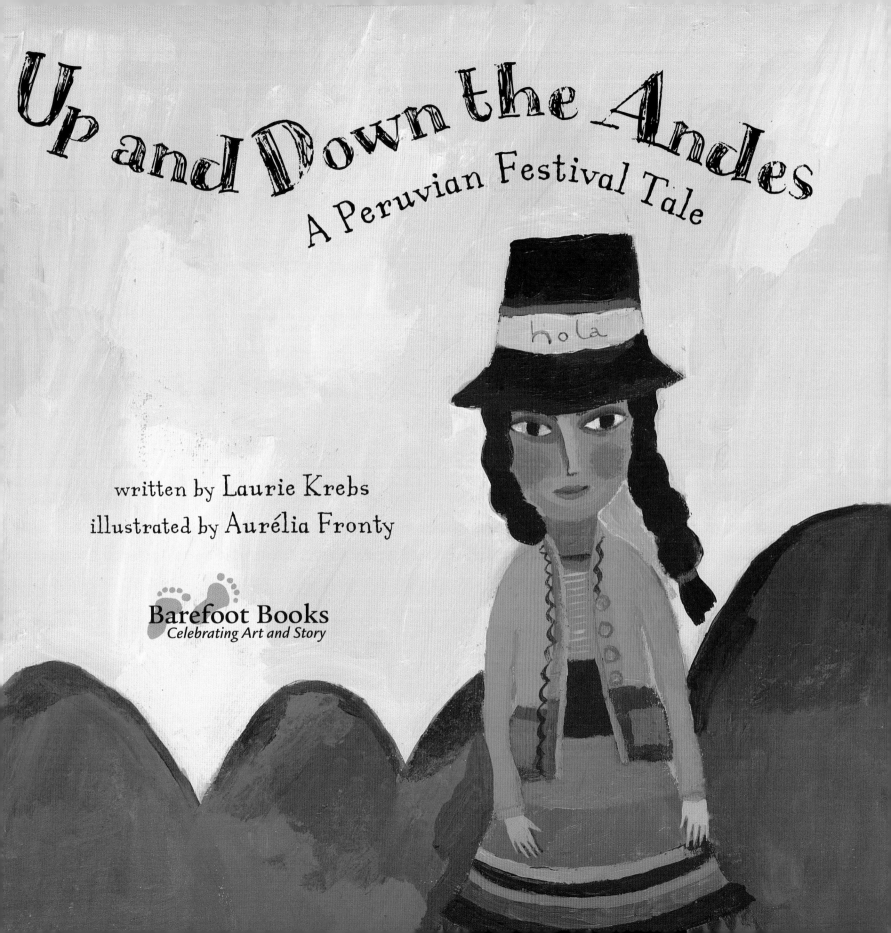

Up and Down the Andes

A Peruvian Festival Tale

written by Laurie Krebs

illustrated by Aurélia Fronty

Barefoot Books
Celebrating Art and Story

The Andes soar to meet the sky.
They plunge to meet the sea.

And up and down the mountain slopes
Live children just like me.

In Lima, José boards a bus,
A long and bumpy ride,

But he protects the headdress
That he places by his side.

Lake Titicaca's boats have docked.
Luisa steps ashore.

She grips the woven family cape
That she will wear once more.

Near Machu Picchu's ancient site,
Along a narrow road,

Ricardo walks beside his mule
And guides its bulky load.

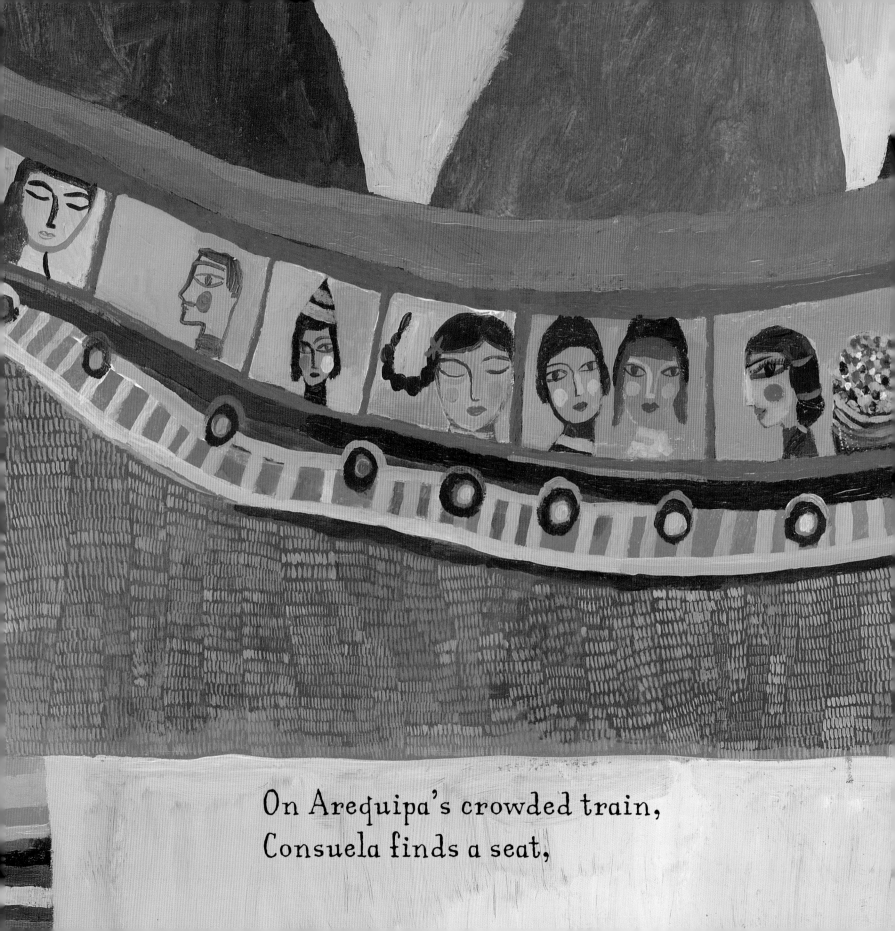

On Arequipa's crowded train,
Consuela finds a seat,

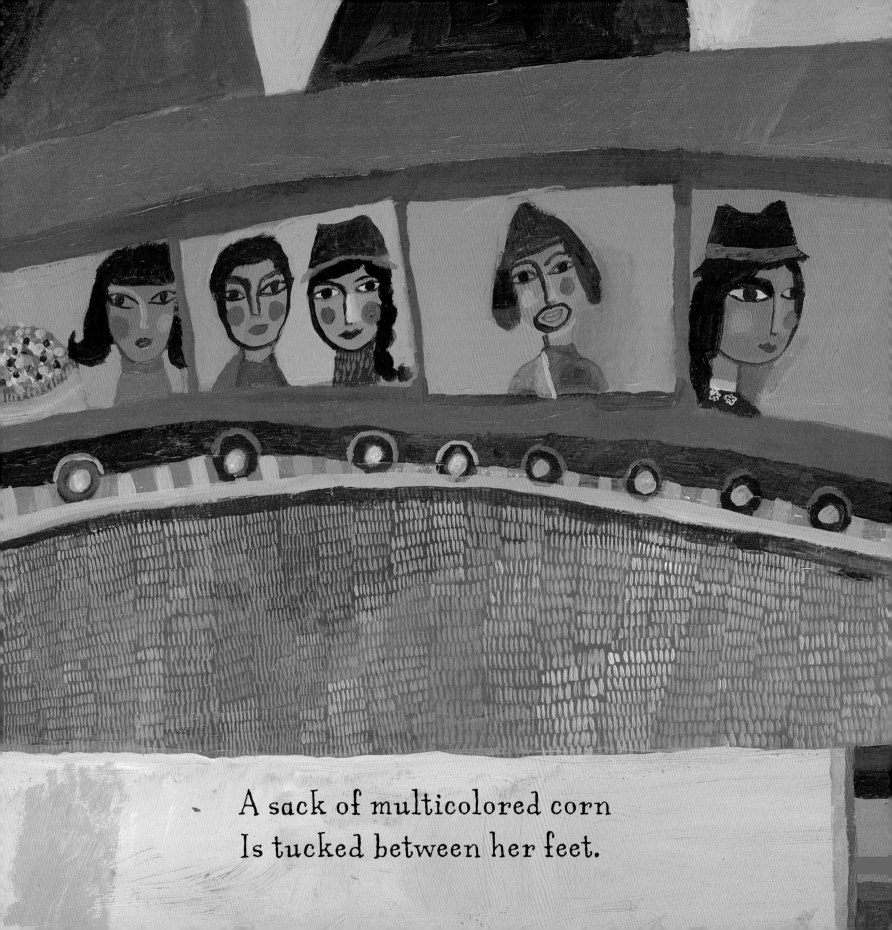

A sack of multicolored corn
Is tucked between her feet.

From Puno, bouncing in the truck
That winds through mountain gaps,

Fidel and Tia, breathless,
Clutch the costumes in their laps.

Up and down the Andes, there's excitement in the air,
And everyone is on their way to Cusco's central square.

The children all are actors and they've come from far and near
To celebrate the festival that's held in June each year.

They change into their costumes and process out to the fort.
The Sun King rises from his throne and stands before the court.

Then speaking to the solemn crowd, he offers thanks and praise
In honor of the Sun God, as was done in ancient days.

That evening, there is partying on every cobbled street.
With laughter, song and dancing to the music's lively beat.

The children celebrate the night with feasting, friends and fun.
The Sun God has returned again! A new year has begun!

The mountains edge the western coast.
They parallel the sea.

And up and down the Andes
There are children just like me.

Inti Raymi: The Festival of the Sun

The festival that is described in this book is Inti Raymi. It is a majestic Inca festival held each year on 24 June to honor the Sun God. Inti Raymi takes place in the city of Cusco, on the winter solstice when the sun is farthest from the Earth. Long ago, the Inca people gathered to pray for the Sun God's return so crops would grow, and they would not go hungry.

Today, Inti Raymi recreates the ancient ceremony as thousands of actors bring the past alive for Cusco's many visitors. The pageantry unfolds in the city square, then everyone processes out of town to the ancient fortress, Sacsayhuaman. High priests, nobles and officials of the court, in elaborate robes, lead the parade. Women in colorful, traditional costumes follow, carrying offerings to honor the gods. The Sun King, resplendent in gold clothing, is carried to the site on a royal litter. After performing age-old rituals, the Sun King climbs to the sacred altar and speaks to the crowd in their native language, Quechua. At sunset, the ceremony ends and everyone returns to Cusco to celebrate the new year.

More Peruvian Festivals

Many festivals in Peru are related to the Christian calendar, but they are often mixed with the ancient religion of the Andean people. Here are a few of the festivals:

Virgen de la Candelaria
(Virgin of Candelaria)
PUNO – FEBRUARY 2

On the shores of Lake Titicaca, a statue of the virgin, Mamapacha Candelaria, is paraded through the city by priests, altar boys and the faithful. Musicians and dancers in brilliant costumes and spectacular masks enliven the festival, once held by ancient people to celebrate the harvest and pay homage to the dead.

El Señor de los Temblores
(Lord of the Earthquakes)
CUSCO – EASTER MONDAY

It is said that in 1650, a painting of Christ on the Cross prevented an earthquake from destroying the city of Cusco. Ever since, on Easter Monday, the image of the Lord of the Earthquakes has been carried through the streets by the faithful, just as the Incas used to parade the mummies of their high priests and rulers.

All Saints' Day
NOVEMBER 1

On this day, people throughout Peru remember loved ones who have died. Families gather at the cemeteries, bringing flowers and food to share

symbolically with the souls of their ancestors. Worshipping the dead was a respected custom in ancient cultures and that tradition, combined with Christian elements, still exists today.

History of Peru

The Inca Empire (1438 - 1532)

The word *Inca* has two meanings – it refers to the emperor himself, but it also means the people he governed. The Incas created the most advanced society in pre–Hispanic America. Their empire began as a small tribe in Cusco, but in time it reached from Ecuador in the north to Chile in the south. The kingdom was divided into four provinces, with a powerful Inca at its head and a governor in each area to oversee local affairs. The royal city of Cusco was the centre of government.

To enlarge his empire, the Inca sent rival leaders luxurious gifts and promises of a better life as his subjects. The rulers usually gave in peacefully since they feared the Inca's mighty army. New subjects were expected to speak the official language, Quechua, and worship the Inca as the earthly child of the Sun God, Inti.

The Ancient People (6000 B.C. - 1448 A.D.)

The earliest people in Peru lived along the coast and in the highlands. At first, they were hunter-gatherers, but over the centuries they banded together into tribes. They became skillful craftsmen, farmers and architects. They were fierce warriors, too. Their written language has not survived, so scientists have used pottery shards and artifacts to learn about their lives.

Colonial Rule (1572 - 1824)

After Pizarro's death, the Spanish Crown sent men called Viceroys to govern Peru. They collected taxes from the people and converted them to Christianity.

The Viceroys were harsh rulers and demanded hard work and obedience from their subjects. During almost three centuries of colonial rule, there were several uprisings among native-born Peruvians who yearned to be free from Spanish control.

The Spanish Conquest (1532 - 1572)

In 1532, Spanish explorers, led by Francisco Pizarro, arrived in Peru. Hearing of the country's vast riches, Pizarro set about gaining control of the Inca Empire. His men were outnumbered by Inca forces but the native people were no match for Spanish guns and horses or Pizarro's clever tricks. One Inca leader after another was captured and killed, so that by 1572, the Inca Empire had been destroyed.

Independence (1824 - the present)

Independence from Spain was granted in 1824, followed by a long period of unrest. Wars, economic problems, unstable governments, terrorist threats and dictatorships plagued the country. In 1979, a new constitution was written and the next year, democratic elections were held. For the first time, there was a peaceful transfer of power from the president to his successor. These are hopeful signs despite the ups and downs of recent governments.

Peoples of Peru

The Chavins (850 B.C. - 300 B.C.)

The Chavin people created beautiful art, textiles and metalwork and were among the earliest groups to hold religious ceremonies.

The Wari (700 A.D. - 1000 A.D.)

The Wari Empire was the first to use military force to spread its power. The Wari built highways, cities and waterways and produced lovely objects in bronze, silver, lapis lazuli and gold.

The Incas (1438 A.D. - 1532 A.D.)

In the brief time they ruled Peru, the Incas accomplished amazing things. Their territory grew from a small region near Cusco to a large empire. They created a network of roads so messengers could carry news quickly from one end of the empire to the other. They built terraced gardens on mountain slopes and performed skull surgery.

The Incas are famous for their architecture and stonework. Without wheels, they moved massive boulders and lifted them on top of one another. Without mortar, they fitted the stones together like puzzle pieces. Their walls and buildings still exist, surviving earthquakes and the passage of time.

Indigenous Peoples Today

An Inca prophecy says, " One day the great sacred birds of the North and the South will fly together." Today, the descendants of the indigenous peoples suffer from poverty and governmental neglect. Although progress is being made, there is still much to do before the sacred birds will fly as one.

Machu Picchu: Old Mountain

Machu Picchu, Peru's most famous site, was built around 1450 A.D. when the Incas were at the height of their power. Set in perfect harmony with its surroundings, nestled between rocky peaks and reached by a serpentine road that winds up from the river below, Machu Picchu's stone buildings defy the imagination.

For several hundred years, the site lay hidden beneath jungle thicket. The Spanish never found it and it seemed all but forgotten by the native people. Then, in 1911, Hiram Bingham, a professor from Yale University, came to Peru searching for Inca ruins. With luck and help from the locals, Bingham stumbled upon the exquisite stonework partly covered by vines and moss. He thought he'd found the Lost City of the Incas. Instead, he had found Machu Picchu, an ancient Inca citadel, now a UNESCO World Heritage site.

The Incas believed their gods lived in nature. To worship them they built temples to the sun, moon and stars; to the mountains and rivers. Buildings were placed so that as the sun rose over the mountain each day, it lit them one by one.

No one knows exactly why Machu Picchu was built, though many legends exist. The ruins remain cloaked in mystery but there is little doubt that it was, and still is, a majestic, sacred place.

The Amazing Andes Mountains

The Andes make up the longest mountain range on Earth, stretching 5,000 miles (8,000 km) along the western coast of South America. They rise steeply from the Pacific Ocean and pass through seven countries: Argentina, Bolivia, Chile, Colombia, Ecuador, Peru and Venezuela. The Andes are the world's second-highest mountains. Only the Himalayas are taller. The Andes' tallest peak, a volcano named Aconcagua, reaches 22,834 feet (6,960 m).

The climate varies from one part of the Andes to another, depending on altitude and location. In the north, the mountains are wrapped in the warm, humid air of the equator. In the south, they are chilled by the damp, cold air of Patagonia. In the central region, the climate is dry, with extreme temperature changes.

For centuries, indigenous peoples have lived in the high regions of the Andes. Farmers still grow crops of corn and potatoes on narrow terraces built into the hillside. Herdsmen raise llamas, alpacas and sheep. These animals can live at high altitudes and provide milk, meat and wool for the local families.

The Andes are rich in minerals. Gold and silver are mined today, just as they were by the indigenous peoples in the 16th century. Copper from Peru and Chile; tin and antimony from Bolivia. Iron ore, lead and zinc are also found in the mountains.

Did You Know?

? The name *Peru* means *Land of Abundance*.

? Peru is the third-largest country in South America, after Brazil and Argentina.

? Lake Titicaca, the world's highest lake, is deep enough for large ships to use. Legend says that the first Inca rose from its depths to create the Inca Empire.

? The Uros Islands on Lake Titicaca are made completely of reeds. They are called *floating islands* because they are anchored to the bottom of the lake.

? The ancient Nazca Lines found in the San José desert are a mystery. These huge drawings of animals, birds and geometric shapes are depicted on the desert floor. No one knows why they are there or what they mean.

? Peru's official language is Spanish, though people in the highlands speak Quechua, the language of the Inca.

Map of Peru

ECUADOR

COLOMBIA

Amazon River

BRAZIL

Andes Mountains

PERU

PACIFIC
OCEAN

* Lima

Machu
Picchu

• Cusco

Arequipa •

Puno •

Lake
Titicaca